**W9-BRI-599**

# BEAR'S ADVENTURE

*Benedict Blathwayt*

ALFRED A. KNOPF · NEW YORK

Copy 1

*For Tom, Harry, Clare,*
*and Flora*

J P

THIS IS A BORZOI BOOK PUBLISHED BY ALFRED A. KNOPF, INC.

Copyright © 1988 by Benedict Blathwayt. All rights reserved under International and Pan-American Copyright Con-
ventions. Published in the United States by Alfred A. Knopf, Inc., New York, and simultaneously in Canada by Random
House of Canada Limited, Toronto. Distributed by Random House, Inc., New York. Published in Great Britain by Julia
MacRae Books, a division of Walker Books, London. Library of Congress Cataloging-in-Publication Data: Blathwayt,
Benedict. Bear's adventure. Summary: A teddy bear left on the beach is swept out to sea and discovers the wonders
on the ocean floor before being returned where he belongs. [1. Teddy bears—Fiction.   2. Ocean bottom—Fic-
tion]   I. Title.  PZ7.B615Be   1988   [E]   88-2696   ISBN 0-394-80568-2   ISBN 0-394-90568-7 (lib. bdg.)
First American Edition        Manufactured in Italy        10  9  8  7  6  5  4  3  2  1

This is Bear.

Bear loved the seashore.

The children built castles for him.

And sometimes they built boats.

But one evening they forgot all about him.

Bear watched the tide come in,
higher and higher.

Soon it was carrying him out to sea.

He grew heavier and heavier...

until he sank down,
down, down, DOWN to the ocean floor.

The tide swept Bear along...

and whirled him around and around

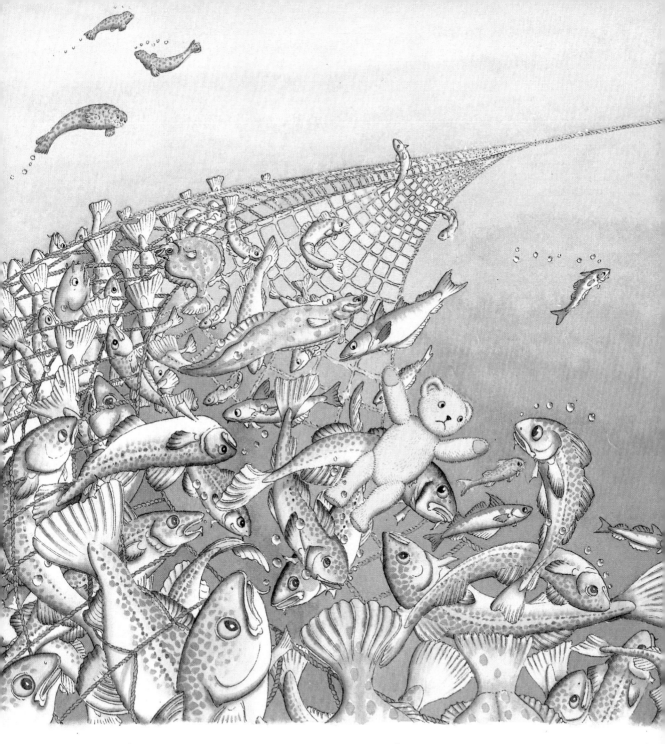

until BUMP! He was caught in a net.

The fishermen picked Bear up,

hung him out to dry…

and sat him in the sun.

OB36

But when the boat docked,
Bear was left all alone.

Not for long!

Higher and higher the sea gull flew...

and then he let Bear drop,

right on top of a huge wave.

Bear was washed ashore.
He heard voices far away.

Then familiar arms
were holding him.
"Bear!" cried a happy voice.
Bear's adventure was over.

JP                                    c.1
Blathwayt, Benedict.
Bear's adventure   $10.99

## DATE DUE

| | |
|---|---|
| APR - 2 1998 | JAN 2 5 2001 |
| MAY 1 - 1998 | FEB 6 2001 |
| | MAR 3 1 2001 |
| | APR 2 8 2001 |
| MAY 3 0 1998 | AUG 1 5 2001 |
| JUN 2 9 1998 | MAY 9 - 2002 |
| AUG 0 8 1998 | APR 0 1 2003 |
| AUG 1 9 1998 | APR 2 3 2003 |
| | MAY 1 3 2003 |
| SEP 8 1998 | NOV 2 6 2003 |
| OCT 1 3 1998 | JAN 2 7 2004 |
| NOV - 4 1998 | FEB 2 4 2004 |
| MAR 1 0 1999 | AUG 1 4 2004 |
| MAY 2 7 1999 | SEP 1 0 2004 |
| AUG 3 1 1999 | SEP 2 1 2004 |
| OCT 2 9 1999 | OCT 2 8 2004 |
| | JAN 0 8 2005 |
| OCT 2 9 1999 | FEB 2 5 2005 |
| DEC 3 2000 | |